MOUNT CLEMENS PUBLIC LIBRARY
3 1509 00126 7494

D1412105

Childrens Press Choice
Distributed by Childrens Press, Chicago.
1988 School and Library Edition

Library of Congress Cataloging-in-Publication Data

Mahy, Margaret.
My wonderful aunt: Book Two / by Margaret Mahy;
Deirdre Gardiner, illustrator.

p. cm. — (My wonderful aunt)
Summary: An episode in the adventurous life of a wonderful aunt, who socializes with zoo animals, sails with a pirate, bakes pies you can wind up like music boxes, and builds a house in the forest.
ISBN 0-516-08912-9 (v. 2)
[1. Aunts—Fiction. 2. Stories in rhyme.] I. Gardiner, Deirdre, ill.
PZ8.3.M278My 1988
[E]—dc19 87-29979
CIP
AC

Created and Designed by Wendy Pye, Ltd.

1 2 3 4 5 6 7 8 9 R 96 95 94 93 92 91 90 89 88

My Wonderful Aunt
Story Two

ISBN 0-516-08912-9
CHILDRENS PRESS CHOICE
A Wendy Pye title selected for educational distribution

Let me tell you a tale
of my wonderful aunt.

She never said, “Won’t!”
and she never said, “Can’t!”

"Try anything once!"
was her regular cry.

"There are lots of adventures
for people who try."

So she worked in a circus
and wrestled a bear,

And swung on trapezes
high up in the air.

She bounced on a tightrope
and juggled with stars,

And whirled herself around
on the parallel bars.

She ran off to sea
with a pirate named Fred,

But came back with diamonds
and parrots instead.

I was gardening one day
when I heard a loud cry,

And there was my aunt
coming out of the sky...

...With two different parachutes
(purple and red),

And a seagull who'd settled
on top of her head.

One day in my kitchen
she started to bake,

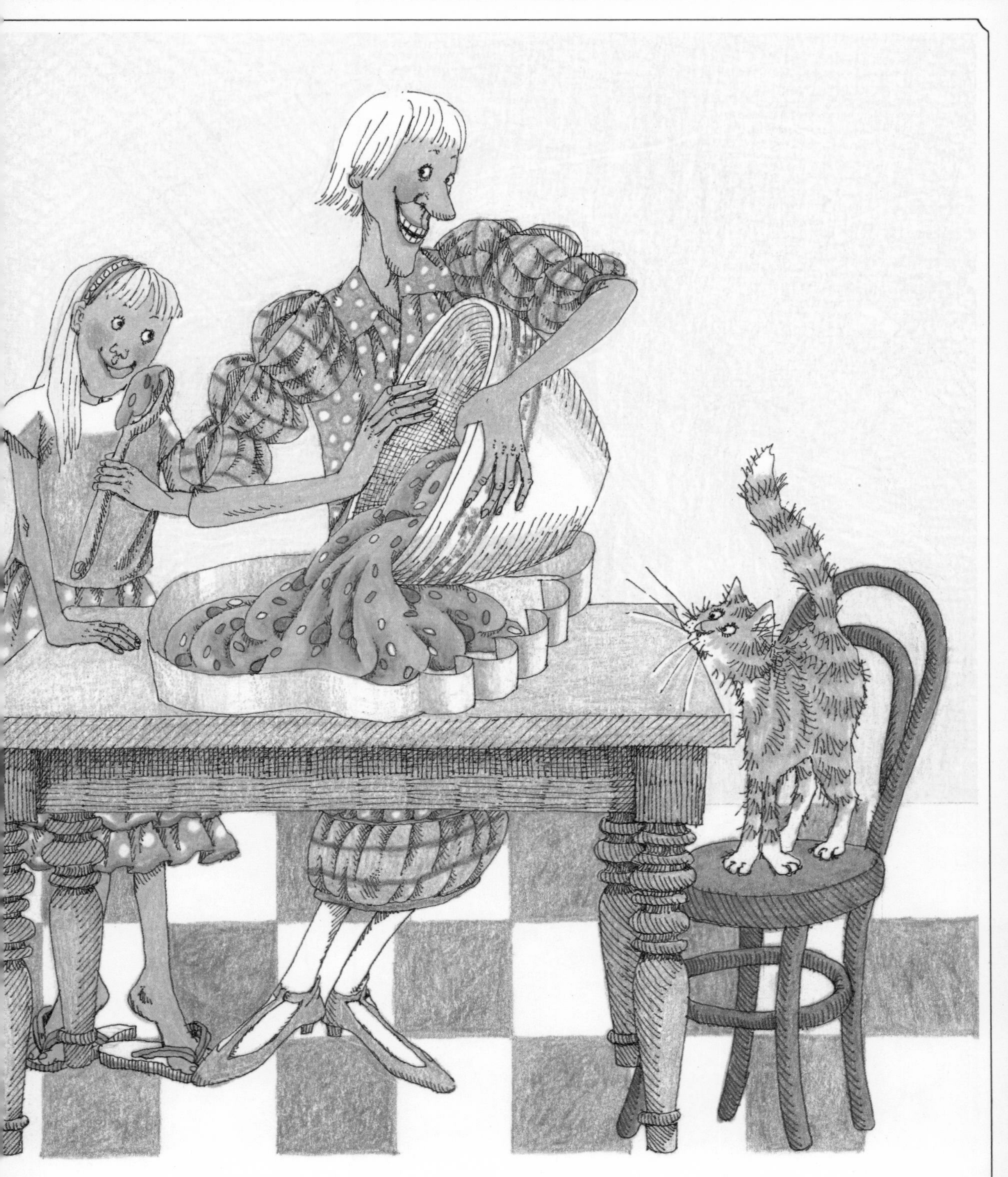

And soon she invented
a new sort of cake.

It was covered in chocolate
and beautifully iced,

And it shouted, "Don't tickle me!" when it was sliced.

She started the octopus
rock and roll band,

So people could dance
up and down on the sand.

“It’s all these adventures which keep me alive!”

Says my aunt who guesses
she's a hundred and five.